the Biggest Little Boy

A Christmas Story

WRITTEN BY
CNN ANCHOR
POPPY HARLOW

ILLUSTRATED BY
RAMONA KAULITZKI

VIKING

On a tree-lined block
in the **BIG**, busy city
lived a little boy named Luca
who loved big things.

BIG trucks . . .

BIG toys . . .

BIG buildings . . .

BIG buses . . .

BIG bulldozers . . .

BIG Saint Bernards . . .

BIG bowls of pasta . . .

BIG statues.
But especially . . .

BIG, BIG trees!

Since he was a little boy, Luca had tried to climb
the biggest tree at Triangle Park.
Each year he made it a little bit higher . . . and higher . . .
but never all the way to the top.
You see, climbing big trees made Luca *feel* BIG.

Luca sighed. "It's not easy being little," Luca said to his parents each night as he lay in bed. In the BIG, busy city, the big grown-ups would bump into him.

They just didn't seem to see him down there.
They were too busy looking up.
It seemed like everything special was up!
So, Luca decided, he would look up, too.

It was nearly Christmas, and more than anything,
Luca wanted a big Christmas tree!
The biggest Christmas tree on his block.
The biggest Christmas tree in the BIG city.

"Can't we cut down the BIG, BIG tree in the middle of Triangle Park?" Luca begged his parents.

"Can't we bring *that* tree home?" he pleaded.

"Maybe we can borrow the one in
the window!" Luca exclaimed.
"We'll know our tree when we see it,"
Luca's parents assured him.

Each day on his walk home from school,
Luca passed the Christmas tree market
on the corner of Cranberry Street.

Fraser firs, balsam firs, white pines.
All lined up from littlest to biggest.

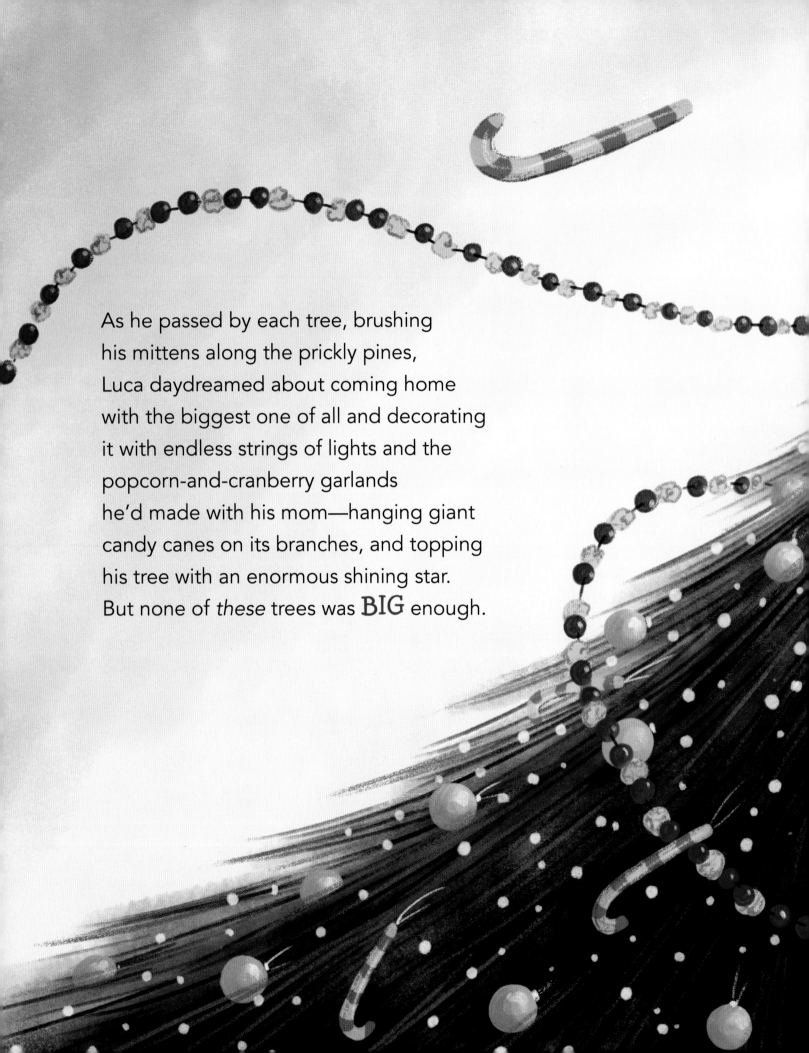

As he passed by each tree, brushing
his mittens along the prickly pines,
Luca daydreamed about coming home
with the biggest one of all and decorating
it with endless strings of lights and the
popcorn-and-cranberry garlands
he'd made with his mom—hanging giant
candy canes on its branches, and topping
his tree with an enormous shining star.
But none of *these* trees was BIG enough.

One crisp late-December afternoon,
after most of his neighbors had trees aglow
in their windows, Luca and his mom walked down
Cranberry Street, past the Christmas tree market.
He was staring *up, up, up* at the not-quite-big-
enough trees when . . .

he tripped!

A little tree had fallen out of its stand and onto the sidewalk.

Luca dusted off his pants and stood up.

He picked up the little tree and plopped it back in its stand.

It wasn't BIG.

It wasn't tall.

Its branches were crooked and needles were missing.

The little tree was anything *but* what Luca had wanted.

But somehow it seemed to be just right.

Perfect, actually, just the way it was.

Luca smiled at the tree. And the tree
seemed to smile back.
"I've found my tree!" Luca exclaimed.
You see, Luca had been so busy
looking up that he had missed the
special things right in front of him.
Special came in every size.

"We never thought anyone would buy this little guy,"
the Christmas tree man, Francois, said to Luca.
"But I'm glad you wanted him."
Beaming, Luca lifted his tree and carried it three long blocks
home all by himself.
That night, Luca would wrap his little tree with garland and
place his favorite baseball cap on the highest branch.

Luca lay in bed, staring up at the
glow-in-the-dark stars on his ceiling.

He felt BIG.
And he was.